The Ugly Duckling

First published in 2005 by
Franklin Watts
96 Leonard Street
London
EC2A 4XD

Franklin Watts Australia
Level 17/207 Kent Street
Sydney
NSW 2000

A CIP catalogue record for this book is available
from the British Library.

ISBN 0 7496 6154 2 (hbk)
ISBN 0 7496 6166 6 (pbk)

Series Editor: Jackie Hamley
Series Advisor: Dr Barrie Wade
Series Designer: Peter Scoulding

Printed in China

The Ugly Duckling

Retold by Maggie Moore

Illustrated by Kay Widdowson

W
FRANKLIN WATTS
LONDON•SYDNEY

Once upon a time,
there was a sad and
lonely duckling.

He was the ugliest
duckling on the pond.

He was big. The other
ducklings were small.

He was grey. The other
ducklings were brown.

"What a strange-looking duckling," laughed the other farm animals.

"Go away, ugly duckling!" they cried. They chased him far away.

The ugly duckling hid in
a reed bank by a river.

He hid in the reeds all
through the summer ...

... and all through
the autumn.

One day, the ugly duckling
saw beautiful, large, white
birds flying in the sky.

"I wish I could be like them," he thought. "Then I would fly away."

But he didn't fly away.
He hid in the reeds all
through the cold winter,
always by himself.

In spring, the ugly duckling
swam through the reeds
into the river.

17

Three beautiful, large, white birds came flying towards him.

18

19

He tried to hide so that
they wouldn't laugh at him.

But it was too late.
They had seen him.

"Why are you all by
yourself?" they asked.

"I was hiding because I'm
so ugly," he replied.

"But you're not ugly.
You're as beautiful as we
are. Look!" they cried.

He looked at himself in the river and saw, not an ugly duckling, but a beautiful, white swan.

"I'm a swan!" he whispered.
"I'm not an ugly duckling
any more!"

"Why don't you come
and join us?" said the
beautiful swans.

Then four beautiful swans
rose up into the air and
flew away together.

31

Leapfrog has been specially designed to fit the requirements of the National Literacy Strategy. It offers real books for beginning readers by top authors and illustrators. There are 31 Leapfrog stories to choose from:

The Bossy Cockerel
ISBN 0 7496 3828 1

Bill's Baggy Trousers
ISBN 0 7496 3829 X

Mr Spotty's Potty
ISBN 0 7496 3831 1

Little Joe's Big Race
ISBN 0 7496 3832 X

The Little Star
ISBN 0 7496 3833 8

The Cheeky Monkey
ISBN 0 7496 3830 3

Selfish Sophie
ISBN 0 7496 4385 4

Recycled!
ISBN 0 7496 4388 9

Felix on the Move
ISBN 0 7496 4387 0

Pippa and Poppa
ISBN 0 7496 4386 2

Jack's Party
ISBN 0 7496 4389 7

The Best Snowman
ISBN 0 7496 4390 0

Eight Enormous Elephants
ISBN 0 7496 4634 9

Mary and the Fairy
ISBN 0 7496 4633 0

The Crying Princess
ISBN 0 7496 4632 2

Jasper and Jess
ISBN 0 7496 4081 2

The Lazy Scarecrow
ISBN 0 7496 4082 0

The Naughty Puppy
ISBN 0 7496 4383 8

Freddie's Fears
ISBN 0 7496 4382 X

Cinderella
ISBN 0 7496 4228 9

The Three Little Pigs
ISBN 0 7496 4227 0

Jack and the Beanstalk
ISBN 0 7496 4229 7

The Three Billy Goats Gruff
ISBN 0 7496 4226 2

Goldilocks and the Three Bears
ISBN 0 7496 4225 4

Little Red Riding Hood
ISBN 0 7496 4224 6

Rapunzel
ISBN 0 7496 6147 X*
ISBN 0 7496 6159 3

Snow White
ISBN 0 7496 6149 6*
ISBN 0 7496 6161 5

The Emperor's New Clothes
ISBN 0 7496 6151 8*
ISBN 0 7496 6163 1

The Pied Piper of Hamelin
ISBN 0 7496 6152 6*
ISBN 0 7496 6164 X

Hansel and Gretel
ISBN 0 7496 6150 X*
ISBN 0 7496 6162 3

The Sleeping Beauty
ISBN 0 7496 6148 8*
ISBN 0 7496 6160 7

Rumpelstiltskin
ISBN 0 7496 6153 4*
ISBN 0 7496 6165 8

The Ugly Duckling
ISBN 0 7496 6154 2*
ISBN 0 7496 6166 6

Puss in Boots
ISBN 0 7496 6155 0*
ISBN 0 7496 6167 4

The Frog Prince
ISBN 0 7496 6156 9*
ISBN 0 7496 6168 2

The Princess and the Pea
ISBN 0 7496 6157 7*
ISBN 0 7496 6169 0

Dick Whittington
ISBN 0 7496 6158 5*
ISBN 0 7496 6170 4

* hardback